This book belongs to:

_____

To Suzie, her girls Hannah and Eliza, and all students of the martial arts.
—O.C.

For my sister, Jessica, and all little girls with big dreams.
—C.C.

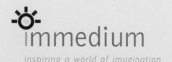

immedium
inspiring a world of imagination

Immedium, Inc.
P.O. Box 31846
San Francisco, CA 94131
www.immedium.com

First hardcover edition published 2007. Second printing March 2012.

Edited by Don Menn
Book design by Stefanie Liang

Printed in Singapore
10 9 8 7 6 5 4 3 2

Library of Congress Cataloging-in-Publication Data

Chin, Oliver Clyde, 1969-
  Julie black belt : the Kung fu chronicles / by Oliver Chin ; illustrated by
Charlene Chua. -- 1st hardcover ed.
    p. cm.
  Summary: Julie is inspired by her film idol to take Kung fu classes, but soon
learns to value the art much more than the color of the belt she might wear.
  ISBN-13: 978-1-59702-009-1 (hardcover)
  ISBN-10: 1-59702-009-5 (hardcover)
  [1. Kung fu--Fiction. 2. Conduct of life--Fiction.] I. Chua, Charlene, ill.
II. Title.
  PZ7.C44235Ju 2007
  [E]--dc22
                                2006101625

ISBN: 978-1-59702-009-1

Julie
BLACK BELT

THE KUNG FU CHRONICLES

Written by Oliver Chin • Illustrated by Charlene Chua

immedium • San Francisco, CA

One day Julie's parents asked her if she wanted to learn something new.

Dad said, "We thought you could try a special sport—it's called kung fu."

KARATE CAMP

"But I know all that martial arts stuff already," replied Julie.

Mom smiled, "Honey, you could become a black belt."

"That's right, just like you-know-who," encouraged her father.

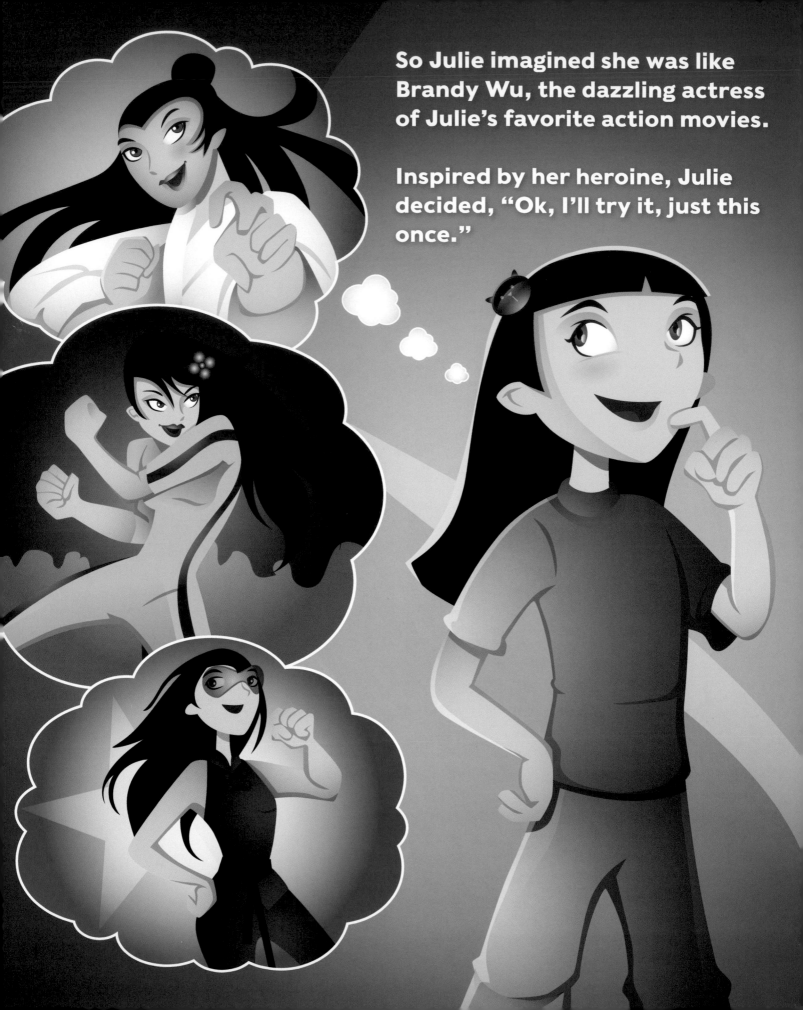

So Julie imagined she was like Brandy Wu, the dazzling actress of Julie's favorite action movies.

Inspired by her heroine, Julie decided, "Ok, I'll try it, just this once."

Her brother Johnny chimed in, "Can I come, too?" His hero was the high-flying superstar Lance Chu.

"Mom and Dad asked me first," insisted Julie. "If you're nice to me, then I might teach you later."

In the meantime, Julie tried on the new uniform that she'd wear to class. "You'll grow into it," winked Dad. But it looked plain without a belt.

"I can't wait to wear a black one," wished Julie.

The following week Mom took Julie to her first class.

SCHOOL OF MARTIAL ARTS

NATIONAL CHAMPIONS KUNG FU

KUNG FU MASTERS GOLD

Brandy XX

Trophies gleamed in the display case. Shiny medals hung from the wall.

Julie marveled, "There's an autographed photo of Brandy Wu!"

As Mom signed Julie up for the "Tiny Tigers" class, Johnny gazed at the children inside the training room.

While she waited, Julie pictured herself meeting the school's teacher.

He would be a sleepy old monk, but be able to lift her with his little finger. Then the master would puzzle her with his bountiful wisdom.

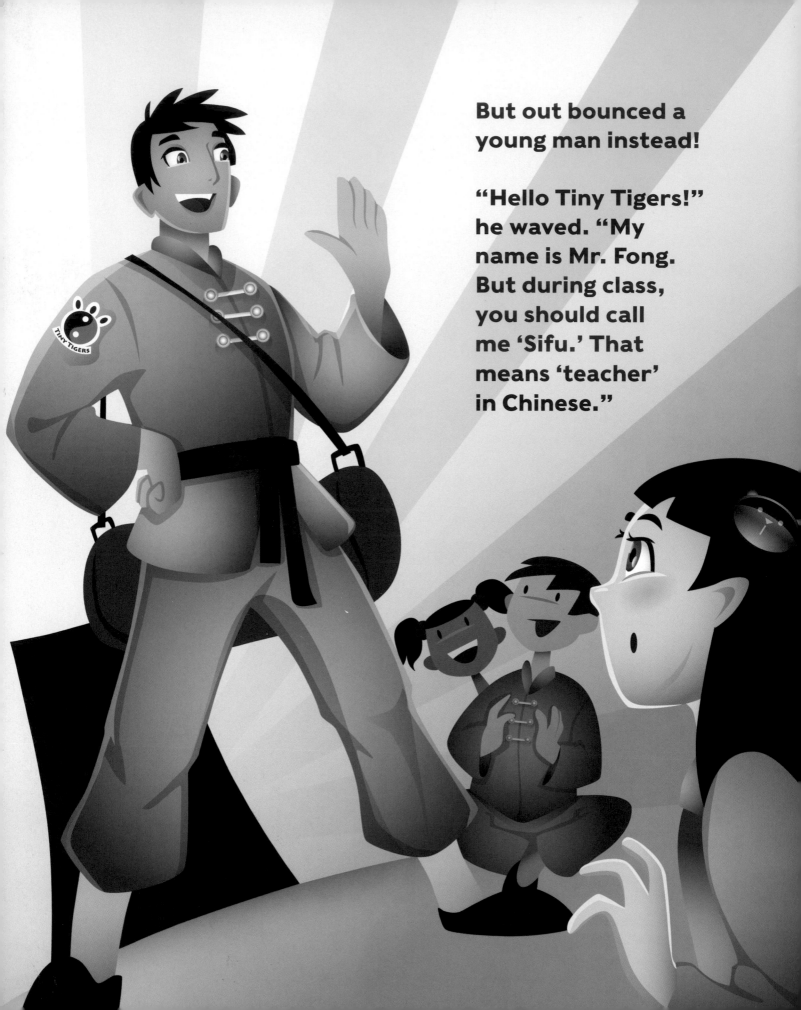

But out bounced a young man instead!

"Hello Tiny Tigers!" he waved. "My name is Mr. Fong. But during class, you should call me 'Sifu.' That means 'teacher' in Chinese."

Mr. Fong pulled a rainbow of belts from his bag. "In kung fu, the color you wear symbolizes your skill," he explained.

"There are White, Yellow, Orange, Green, Blue, Brown, and Black." But he put each belt back until just the white was left.

Then Mr. Fong declared, "Every beginner has a white belt and must work their way up."

"Wait a minute, Mr. Fong, I mean Sifu. Why can't I wear a black belt now?" demanded Julie.

"It takes a lot of practice to earn each belt," answered Sifu. "Getting better at kung fu takes time and hard work. But if I can do it, you can, too. So let's get started!"

The first lesson was learning how to bow and salute. Sifu explained, "It is important to greet each other with respect."

But Julie asked, "When do we get to the real action?"

"Remember kung fu is about self-defense," emphasized Sifu. "When you know how to protect yourself, then you know how to behave at all times."

Julie recalled that's exactly what Brandy Wu would do.

Next Sifu showed his students how to stand like a horse and stretch like a cat.

"Oh anybody can do that," laughed Julie, since she had mastered much harder moves in games before.

At home Julie admired Brandy Wu more than ever. She would fly and fall like a graceful dancer, and never seem to get a scratch.

But it wasn't as easy as it looked, especially for Julie.

Twice a week Julie would go to kung fu class.

But amid the loud shouting and clapping, she couldn't help noticing rounder kids kicking higher, smaller ones whirling faster, and older ones punching harder.

One day, tired and sore from the twirling and tumbling, Julie sighed, "A gold belt isn't worth all this trouble."

Just then Sifu whispered in her ear, "A black belt is just a white belt that doesn't quit."

On the way home, Johnny wondered, "How many years does it take to get a black belt?"

Julie responded, "I don't know. But Brandy Wu never gives up, and neither will I."

Just for fun, Sifu took the Tiny Tigers on field trips.

There they learned how to dance like lions, think deep thoughts in a quiet garden, and exercise with grownups in the park.

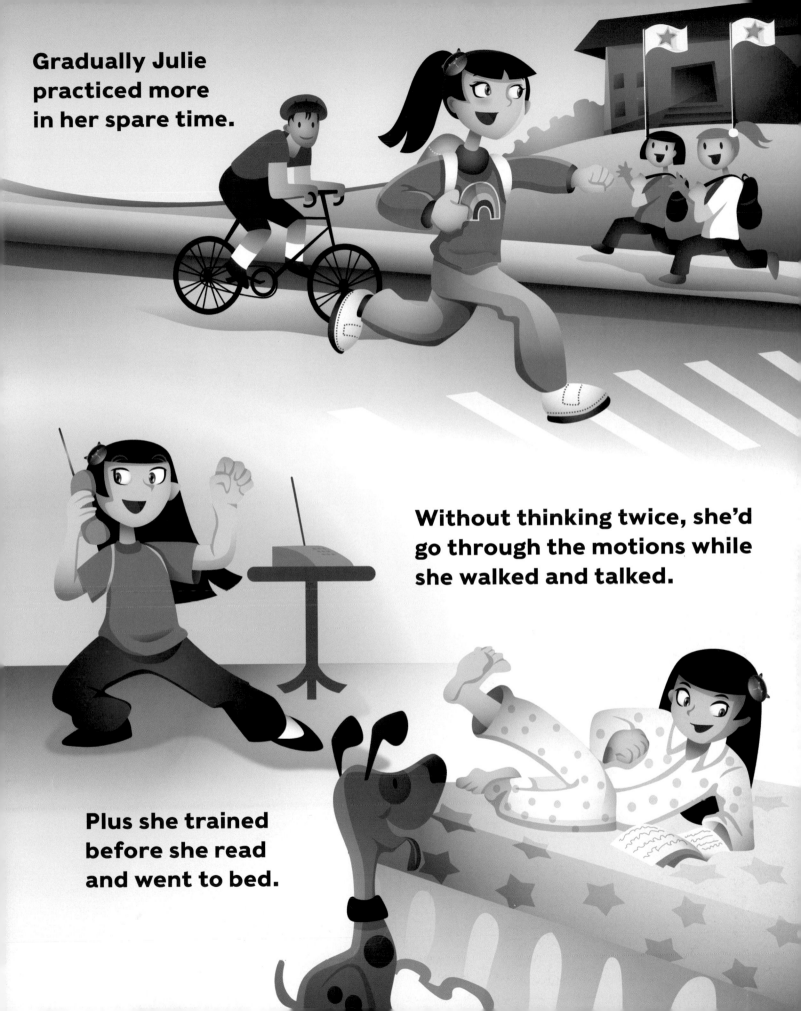

Gradually Julie practiced more in her spare time.

Without thinking twice, she'd go through the motions while she walked and talked.

Plus she trained before she read and went to bed.

Soon Julie looked forward to learning new moves and combining them with the ones she already knew. In class, she tugged, dodged, and jumped with more enthusiasm than ever before.

Then one day Julie asked Sifu, "What do we do next? This is getting really fun."

YELLOW BELT TESTS!

NEXT WEEK!

Sifu smiled, "The yellow belt test is coming up next week. I think you should get ready for it."

Julie had forgotten all about getting another belt!

In the backyard Julie carefully went through her drills.

As she balanced, she felt more confident than when she first began months ago. From the window Johnny shouted, "I hope your training pays off!"

"Watch me and learn, Young Cricket," replied Julie and motioned for her brother to come outside.

LANCE

Johnny joined her on the grass, and Julie took a time out to teach him from the beginning.

Finally, the day of the test came. Mom, Dad, and Johnny took their seats.

YELLOW BELT TEST

Soon Sifu barked instructions to the Tiny Tigers who were trying to earn a yellow belt. Julie was next in line!

Julie closed her eyes, inhaled deeply, and breathed out her worries. Then she swept through the air with spinning arms and springing legs.

Julie felt like a softly floating feather that could suddenly change into a hard arrowhead.

Only when the exam was finished, did she become nervous, as she awaited Sifu's decision.

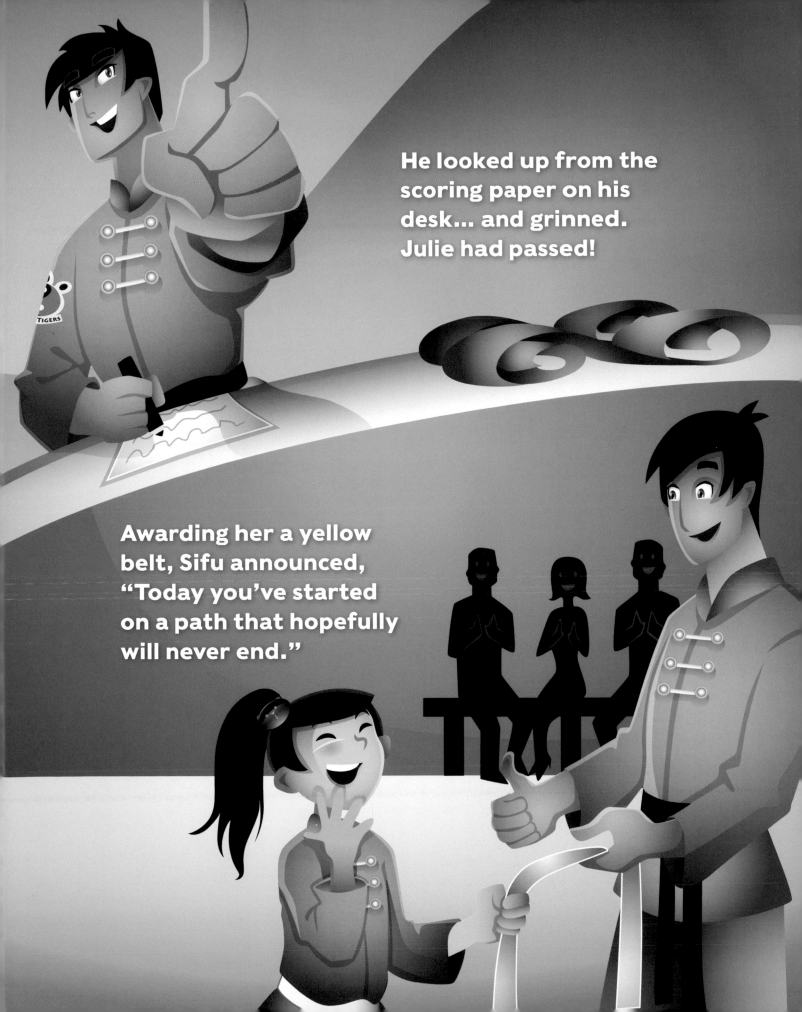

He looked up from the scoring paper on his desk... and grinned. Julie had passed!

Awarding her a yellow belt, Sifu announced, "Today you've started on a path that hopefully will never end."

It was an auto-graphed photo from Brandy Wu!

To my biggest fan, Congratulations, Julie!

Brandy Wu

Black belt here we come!

INTRODUCING STORY APPS

Enjoy your favorite immedium stories on your iPad!

FEATURES INCLUDE:

- "Read To Me" highlights the words to improve reading skills

- "I Can Read" allows reading at your own pace

- Individual and multiple words can be selected for playback

- Interactive surprises and hidden objects on every page

- Original music and professional narration

- Auto Play lets you watch the story like a movie

"*The Year of the Dragon* is another top notch animated title from Mobad Media, just in time for Chinese New Year! It features scenes that tilt for a 3D effect when the device is moved, lots of interactivity and a story that will engage kids from start to finish. It even includes some great extras, featuring information about the Chinese Zodiac and a series of hidden coins children can find while exploring each page."

★ ★ ★ ★ ⯪
—*Digital Storytime*

Editor's Choice:
"Children and parents alike are going to fall in love with *Billie The Unicorn*. Between the gorgeous artwork, 3D effects, and the charming story, *Billie The Unicorn* will become a favorite for every family who downloads it. The artwork alone in this book is worth adding to the library, but the story makes it that much better."
—*AppTudes*